WIFE OF THE WIND

For my beloved husband, John,
and my precious girls, Aly and Emily

KATE NICHOLAS
ILLUSTRATED BY THERESA NICHOLAS

ISBN: 1503318419
ISBN 13: 9781503318410

CHAPTER ONE

On the top of a mountain in a small, grey stone cottage overlooking the sea lived a beautiful young maiden. She was pale as snow and tall and graceful like a dancer, and she had long, raven-black hair that whipped around her face when the wind blew. The maiden's name was Eleri.

Eleri was happy in her own way. She loved the way the sea beat on the rocks below the cottage, sending spray as white as ice into the air outside her windows. At night the water was dark and mysterious, and she imagined that the sea talked to her, whispering its secrets to her as she slept.

Most of all she loved the wind—the wild breath that would scream around her house, blowing down the chimney pot, rattling at the windows, begging to be let in to play with her long, raven-black tresses. Sometimes when the wind called her, she would open the door and walk to the edge of the cliff. The wind would then lift her up and cradle her.

Indeed, her spirit was as wild as that of the wind's. Eleri's mother and father had passed away when she was little more than a child. Her parents had been humble people, who had left her alone with just a small parcel of land on the steep hillside, and a few animals who grazed on the sparse grass. And so Eleri worked to feed and

CHAPTER ONE

clothe herself with what little the small farm provided. As she grew she was so alone that sometimes she fancied that the wind was her only friend. She looked forward to the nights when the wind howled, when his song would weave around the house and he would dance with the trees and the waves.

But as the years went by, and Eleri blossomed into womanhood, she began to wonder what lay beyond the sea outside her window. She imagined lands across the ocean where the air was rich with spices, the sun beat down on golden sands, and women draped themselves in silks of scarlet. She began to tire of the sea and its secrets and of her little grey cottage. She longed for new sights.

Now when the wind came to call, she would cry, "Take me with you. Carry me to Zanzibar, to Marrakech, to lands I've not yet met." But the wind only whistled, tapping at her windows, before it left her alone yet again.

Eleri began to wish that she could be more like the wind—free to roam the world at will.

Once when the wind came, she pleaded with him again, saying, "Let me come with you, and I will stay with you always. Together we will see the world, and you will never again roam alone. Take me with you, and I will become the wife of the wind. Where the wind goes, I go."

Hearing this, the wind's heart raced, for he loved the maiden with the raven hair with all his heart. This time, he did not tap at the window. He burst into the house and carried her out of the little cottage and high up into the night sky.

Higher and higher towards the stars he carried her. As she looked down, she could see her little, grey stone cottage, the windows and doors blown open to the sea air. She could hear the waves playing with the rocks, and as the wind sang a song of great joy, she whispered good-bye to her home.

The wind carried her far away from her blue-and-grey world. By night, they crossed the ocean, whipping up waves as high as mountains and tossing the little fishing boats in the air like flotsam. By day, they crossed great deserts, sending clouds of sand into the sky. So wild were the storms that they would sometimes block out the sun.

And there below, through a haze of sand, Eleri sometimes glimpsed a flash of red silk whipping around the face of a woman as she bowed her head against the storm to fetch water from a distant well.

Then there were the great cities and markets, or "souks." The wind rushed through the narrow crowded alleyways, beating the brilliantly coloured woven carpets hanging from the rafters; rattling the copper pots and pans on the merchants' stalls; and taking the finely ground spices—cumin, turmeric, and saffron—and tossing the scents in the air to be carried onto distant lands. Later that day, somewhere below, a fisherman stopped while pulling in his nets and wondered at the beautiful aromas that wafted on the breeze.

On and on they travelled, the wind and his wife. For many days and many months, they explored, until one day they came upon a fabulous palace. At every corner of the palace rose a great tall tower, at the top of which sat a small room with a balcony. The walls of the palace appeared to be made of lace that shimmered in the breeze. Inside, every surface was set with precious stones that glinted in the light of one hundred lanterns. The deep-blue ceilings were inlaid with diamonds and gold, which shone like the stars in the night sky.

The wind flitted from room to room while Eleri wandered, amazed by the beauty of the palace. It was so very different from her little cottage, and she wondered who would live in a place of such splendour.

She begged the wind, saying, "Please, can I stop awhile in this place? We have travelled for many a long day and many a long night, and now I would like to rest awhile."

Of course the wind could not stop, but he loved Eleri so much that he agreed. He would continue on his way and return in one year and one day. When she was rested, they would carry on their journey together. The wind bid his love farewell and rose up into the sky, climbing higher and higher until he was hidden by the clouds.

CHAPTER TWO

Far below, Eleri stood alone in an open courtyard, watching as rain drops dotted the desert floor, stirring the dust for the first time in many moons, and knew that the wind cried for her.

And as he cried, the desert sprang to life all around her, with green shoots thrusting their way towards the scorching sun. For a desperate moment, she wondered if she had done the right thing, but her thoughts were interrupted by a voice, strong and commanding.

"Who is it who has made this miracle, bringing water and life to the desert?" demanded the sultan as he strode into the courtyard. He was a fine, handsome man, with gentle black eyes that shone like a great bird's but were softened with laughter lines, and his skin was polished like ebony and wrapped in white silks embroidered with gold.

He beckoned the maiden who had brought the rain to follow him. As he strode off into the coolness of the palace, she hurried after him, scurrying down long corridors, turning this way and that. At last they stopped before a beautifully carved dark wooden door. There he left her, in silence, with nothing but a nod.

She cautiously opened the door and peered inside, and her breath was taken away. Every wall looked like finely drawn lace, the delicate veil letting in shafts of sunlight that created golden patterns on the white marble floor. Up close, she could see that the lace was actually made of marble carved so finely that it seemed impossible that it could have been shaped by human hands. Beyond the walls she could see yet another courtyard. This one was painted in brilliant turquoise and inlaid with hand-painted tiles that shimmered like the tail of a peacock.

In the centre of the room stood a vast silk-covered bed strewn with cushions of every colour, richly embroidered with golden thread. Alongside, a chair was draped with a dress of such dazzling splendour that it nearly blinded Eleri.

As dusk fell, the summons of a gong shattered the peace of the palace. A young servant came for her and led her from the sanctuary of her beautiful room and down through a maze of darkened corridors until they came upon a great hall of pillars. Behind every pillar stood a servant holding up a flaming torch that illuminated the scene within.

As her eyes became used to the light, Eleri marvelled as dancing girls whirled before her like tornadoes wrapped in clouds of light chiffon material. The tables were covered in white linen and laden with all kinds of exotic fruits—mango, kumquat, papaya, and pineapple—as well as roasted mutton, camel, and peacocks on platters of gold. Great round breads were broken by the bejewelled hands of courtiers who sat to one side or the other of the sultan.

The great man now beckoned Eleri to sit beside him and raised a golden goblet of wine in honour of her arrival and the miracle of the rain she brought with her. Then he handed her a single flower, red as blood, which had grown unexpectedly from the sand. Truly she was a blessing to those who lived in the dry desert.

It was a night unlike any that Eleri had imagined, even in her wildest dreams when she lived alone on the mountaintop, yearning for the sun. The first light of day had stolen over the sand dunes before she made her way back to her room.

The next night there was another great banquet, this time in honour of a Bedouin chief, the leader of a wandering tribe passing through the sultan's land. Through the lace-like marble of her walls, Eleri watched as the Bedouins, their faces protected from the sand by white scarves, made their way across the dunes towards the palace, their camels padding softly and silently across the sand. She watched in wonder as they pitched their great tents made of goat hides and strained her eyes to see the riches inside.That night, unfamiliar music wove its way through the corridors, as the Bedouins sang, played and danced to a strange beat.

During the days, she wandered through the palace corridors, which were so cool and silent that all she could hear were the sounds of her own footsteps. Sometimes she would wander beyond the palace walls just to feel the heat of the sand beneath her feet. She would watch the horizon for the merchants' camel trains, laden with rich silks and spices to sell and bringing yet more visitors to the palace. Then every night, she would find a robe even more splendid than before laid out in her room, and she would sit at the sultan's right hand for yet another feast.

As the days turned to weeks, the sultan became more and more enchanted by Eleri. She fascinated him with tales of her travels and of lands he could only imagine. Yet even his imagination failed him when she described her little stone cottage and the wildness of the cold, dark sea. The sultan had been born in a land of light, where the sun was so strong that even the brilliant colours of the maiden's robes paled in comparison, so he could never imagine her world so grey and blue.

Little by little, the sultan began to love the maiden who had entered his world so mysteriously.

Then one evening, the sultan ordered the cook to prepare a feast grander than any tasted before. He ordered his servants to hang the rooms with great tapestries laced with golden thread. And there he waited for the maiden, still as a statue amidst the light of one hundred candles.

As dusk fell, Eleri appeared before him. First he poured her wine as red as rubies, and then he fed her sweetmeats more delicious than anything she had tasted before. Finally he declared his love for her and asked for her hand in marriage.

He held his breath, waiting for her answer. But then Eleri spoke, softly like a summer breeze, saying, "Oh my lord, you do me a great honour, and I admire you above all men. But I have done you a dishonour. I did not mean to keep it a secret and should have told you when we first met."

She faltered, and the sultan urged her to speak again.

"What is this secret that burns within you?" he asked.

"I can never be your wife because I am already spoken for," she whispered.

The sultan jumped to his feet. "Who has spoken for you? What kind of man would win the heart of such a beautiful maiden and then leave her to the cruel desert? I will fight him."

But Eleri told him, "He is not a man, my lord. You cannot fight the wind."

The sultan was puzzled. "The wind? You tell me that you are the wife of the wind?"

"That is so, my lord, and I am a faithful wife and will remain so until the wind passes this way again," she replied. Bewildered, the sultan sank back down onto his ottoman. Eleri bowed her head and quietly slipped away from his sight.

CHAPTER THREE

But the sultan was not to be so easily put off. He had set his heart on the mysterious maiden, and he did not fear the wind.

The desert had lain still for many a long day. No sandstorms had been stirred to block out the sun, and so he had forgotten the power of the wind. The sultan also had his own power, for he was wise in the ways of magic.

And so the sultan used his power and created a magic potion guaranteed to make whoever drank it love the maker with all his or her heart, and to forsake all others. That evening, as Eleri joined him to eat, he slipped the potion into her goblet.

As she drank, she forgot her grey days. She forgot her great journey and the wind. All she could think about was the sultan, and he was happy.

Three days later, they were married with a quiet ceremony in the palace courtyard, with only the household staff to witness the sultan's unholy bonding to the wife of the wind. As she said her vows, Eleri felt a momentary sense of foreboding, and as the sultan looked down on her furrowed brow, his thoughts turned to the wind. But the sultan's love conquered caution and as he smiled down at his bride, her fears faded.

The following day, and every day after that, they rose at dawn and rode out while the sands were still cool. And when the heat of the day came, they sat in the shade of his palace, whiling away the time with games and dances.

It was an easy life, and the maiden was happy. But sometimes in the middle of the night, she would be haunted by a vague feeling that she had forgotten something important. The memory was too strong to ignore, but too fleeting to grasp. In the daylight, she would struggle to recall the memory that had kept her from sleep, and wondered at its meaning, but it was no use.

After many months, Eleri gave birth to a son, Galen, a boy of such beauty and perfection that he delighted all who set their eyes on him. His eyes were blue grey, like the sea that the maiden had grown up with, his hair golden like the sands amongst which she now lived, and his skin a golden brown like burnished teakwood.

His temper was as sweet as his appearance. Even when he was only a few days old, he fixed his eyes on his mother's face and lay quietly without crying. In the middle of the night, his crying sounded like singing.

The sultan was so proud of the boy that he thought his heart would burst with happiness. He pushed the guilt he sometimes felt late at night to the back of his mind, for it was then that he remembered his perfect happiness owed more to magic than nature. He also chose to forget the wind and its ways.

But the wind had not forgotten. For many months, the wind had made its lonely way around the world, hurrying in the seasons. In his loneliness, he brought misery to many as storms raged. The wind did not mean to be unkind, but his power was great, and as his emotions

waxed and waned so did the weather. But as time progressed, and he counted down the days until he saw his love again, the raging storms turned to refreshing breezes.

Finally one year and one day had passed, and the wind raced through the night sky to greet his love. As dawn broke, the wind looked down on the lace walls of the palace. There, alone in one of the beautiful courtyards and perched on the edge of a fabulously carved fountain, he spied the maiden. Prince Galen lay in her arms, gazing into her face with his tiny fingers tangled in her raven hair.

In the sky above, the wind sensed the power of the sultan's magic and howled in despair. Nearly mad with grief, the wind rushed down and burst through the wooden gates of the palace. As he rushed through the corridors, muslin veils were torn from stone archways and tossed and carried on the tide of air. Sand, taken from the desert outside, stung the eyes and faces of the servants, blasting away the beautiful carvings in every corner of the palace. As the sultan heard the wind wail, he trembled.

Finally the wind came upon the courtyard and Eleri, who, instead of greeting her husband, cowered and shielded her baby son from his anger. Her face showed no sign that she remembered him. No memory of their love glimmered in her eyes. The wind saw only her fear.

The sultan rushed to Eleri's side, and together they hid behind the stone walls. But the wind could still sense the power of the sultan's magic, and it was at that moment that he realised the love between him and the maiden had been forgotten. The wind rose up from the palace courtyard into the blue sky above, carrying the desert sand up into a great whirlwind.

The sultan and his family huddled together as they watched the dangerous spiral of earth and air race across the desert and disappear into the distance. Then, their baby's cry pulled their attention back from the horizon, and the wind was left to make his lonely way to around the world.

CHAPTER FOUR

The young Prince Galen grew into a strong and healthy boy. The beauty and gentleness that he had displayed in his first hours of life continued to delight Eleri and the sultan. His laughter and the sound of his first uncertain steps rang through the palace, bringing a new sense of life.

But as the months passed, this perfect existence became marred by the wind, or rather, the lack of it. For since that fateful day when the wind had lost his love, he had wandered far from the desert that the maiden now called home.

In his anger and confusion, he had turned the world on its head. Where there had been sun, now the lands were lashed with blizzards of ice that froze the grapes on the vine and turned the days of songs and wine to those of tears. The oceans rose like the great peaks of the Atlas Mountains, and many honest sailors lost their lives at sea.

And while the earth paid for his pain, Eleri grew weak from the endless heat that rose from the desert floor and hung like a silver mist, undisturbed by even the slightest breeze. With every breath, the hot air burned her lungs, and what she suffered, her child suffered one hundredfold. Galen's laughter no longer rang through the halls, and his first words died on his lips as he lay in the heat. He did not even have the energy to brush the flies from his face.

So great was the wind's grief that he was blind to all the suffering he caused. But one day, a vulture, the bird of death, passed his way.

"Where are you hastening to, bird of doom?" asked the wind.

"Ah, I have an appointment at the palace of the great sultan," replied the vulture. "They say his child is sick with the heat and will not last the night. His mother does not sleep but fans his face all day for want of a breeze, but it is not enough. So I must fly."

The words of the bird pierced the heart of the wind like an arrow. "How could I have caused my love and her child to suffer? This tragedy is not of her making. I must save the boy."

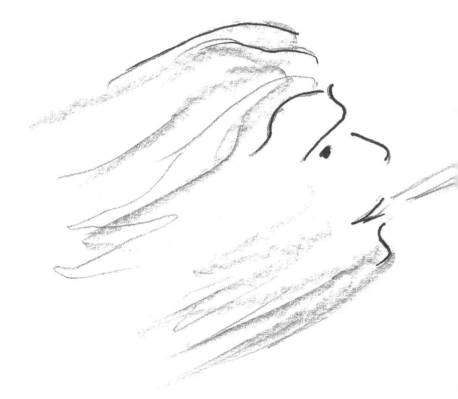

Once again, the wind passed over the palace, but this time he brought the breath of life. As the boy felt the soft breeze on his face and the heat lifting from his brow, he raised his head to see who had brought relief. He thought he heard a sigh, but there was no one there.

Every night, the wind watched over Galen and rejoiced in his recovery and the light of happiness that now shone in the eyes of Eleri. As the days passed, the wind came to love the boy as much as the maiden. He saw that he was an innocent who knew nothing of the ways of the wind.

The wind also brought presents that made the boy smile. Some nights, he would carry perfumes from the east—deep, rich musk and sandalwood scents that hung in the air like a fragrant cloud. Sometimes he brought the earthy aromas of turmeric and saffron from the markets that Eleri had loved so well.

On these nights, he thought he saw a glimmer of recognition in her eyes. As he passed by, scattering these strange scents, she would stop what she was doing and stand silent and still, as if searching her memory for something treasured but now long gone.

It was then that the wind knew what he must do. He remembered the cold, grey land that he had taken her from, which was so very different from that in which she and her son now lived. He vowed that he would once again turn the world on its head—this time, to make her remember.

CHAPTER FIVE

The sultan and Eleri were playing with their son in the sun when they heard a roar and felt freshness in the air. Eleri put her hand to her face and felt a fine spray. Putting her hand to her mouth, she tasted salt.

Then they saw the impossible: a great wall of water moved slowly across the desert. A giant wave, more than one hundred feet tall came out of the sky and bore down upon the sands.

The grey-blue wall of water moved across the endless dunes until the waters crashed onto the sand, sending clouds of sea mist into the air above the palace. Then slowly, the storm waters calmed until a great expanse of sea lay before the maiden.

As the waves lapped at her feet, she breathed deeply, drawing in the sweetness of the sea air. With her child at her side, she watched the two worlds meet—the cold blue grey of the sea and the pale gold of the desert. And at last she remembered the glorious freedom of her life with the wind, and she laughed for joy.

Prince Galen clung to her skirts and looked on in wonder as she once again raised her arms to the wind. The sultan hung his head in shame as he remembered the magic he had used to bind the maiden to him.

Then the wind spoke with a voice of thunder, saying, "Wife of the wind, I have come for you." At these words, the sultan trembled in fright.

The young prince, however, stood firm against the might of the wind. He remembered the nights that the wind's gentle breezes had chased away death and was not afraid. He held up his hands to feel the sea breezes and paddled his toes in the clear blue waters. Only Eleri stood still as stone on the seashore that had appeared in the desert.

The world seemed to stand still before she finally spoke, saying with tears in her eyes, "I am so sorry, but I can no longer follow you, my love."

The only sound that could be heard across the miles of sea and sand was the sigh of the wind for, as he looked down on the sultan and his child, he realised that Eleri's heart was no longer his alone.

And so it was that, with sadness and great love, the wind released his wife to live life in the desert—but not totally, for a heart that longs for the unknown can never be completely still.

Eleri mourned for the wind, but in time forgave the sultan because she realised that he had cast the spell for love. And so together they went on to raise a son as brave as a lion, kind and just, but with his mother's spirit.

And the wind, who had grown to love the boy as his own, would return from his travels to teach Prince Galen about the marvels of foreign lands and endless oceans. As spring turned to summer and autumn to winter, he would breeze into the palace creating anew a sense of wonder at the world.

As he grew, Galen learned to gallop across the dunes with the wind in his hair and to cross the ocean waves with the breeze filling his sails. His life went on to be one of great adventure—but that is another story.

And while Prince Galen was growing, the wind watched over Eleri. As the years rolled by, he saw her raven-black hair turn silver, and her son become a fine young man. Until finally the day came when Eleri realised she was too tired to continue walking the earth.

The sultan's bright eyes were now dimmed as well, but Eleri saw her love reflected in them and in the eyes of her son, and so she was at peace. The wind, who had waited for her so patiently, knew that his wait was over at last.

One clear night in summer, when the wind had chased away the clouds that lay between the earth and the stars, Eleri lay down her head to dream. Slowly and softly, her breathing stilled, and her spirit left her body and soared once more into the sky, free now to roam with the wind until the end of time.

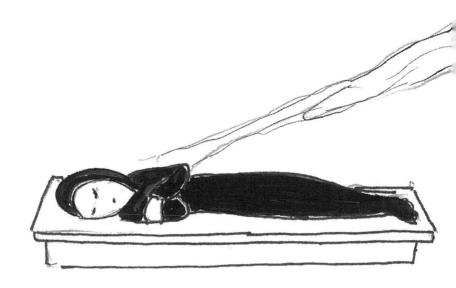

AUTHOR BIOGRAPHY

K ate Nicholas is a British writer with over twenty years' experience writing for national and local newspapers and editing business magazines. She currently heads up global communications for a leading international humanitarian agency. She has travelled extensively in Europe, Asia, and Africa and previously lived in Australia. She now lives in Buckinghamshire with her husband and two daughters.

Theresa Nicholas is an artist and author who lives and works in Corfu. Published works include *Suntouched: A Dark Comedy on a Greek Island*, *Pippa's Ark* and *Corfu Sketches: A Thirty-Year Journey*.

53596833R00024

Made in the USA
Charleston, SC
16 March 2016